WHEN YOU LOVE
YOU MUST DEPART

ALINA REYES
When You Love You Must Depart

*translated from the French
by David Watson*

Methuen

To Olivier

First published as *Quand tu aimes, il faut partir* in 1993
by Éditions Gallimard, Paris

First published in Great Britain in 1995
by Methuen London
an imprint of Reed Consumer Books Ltd
Michelin House, 81 Fulham Road, London SW3 6RB
and Auckland, Melbourne, Singapore and Toronto

A CIP catalogue record for this book
is available from the British Library
ISBN 0 413 68700 7

Phototypeset by Intype, London
Printed and bound in Great Britain
by Mackays of Chatham PLC

1

What I like is departing, taking the road. Space, the present, forgetting.

The road is me, it is a snake; the road stretched out behind me is my former skin which I am sloughing off, still. The road is my life, continually shedding my layers of wrapping, getting out of myself to be reborn bright and new, giving life to the unknown who keeps vigil inside me, waiting for her liberation.

The road is a bit like love: you feel yourself set off, then nothing else matters except being there, in the process of experiencing it, heading for a destination that often has no name, that may recede or change as you approach it, a destination whose interest lies in never being final, a destination which is not in the direction of death, but, in its movement of perpetual resurrection, the very glorification of life.

I set off this morning. It was the telephone which woke me up. I didn't answer it. On the answerphone, Oscar asked if I was asleep, then added a tender word.

I was warm, too warm. I kicked the quilt down to the end of the bed, and pulled off my nightshirt and threw it on the ground in one movement.

Down below is the Cité des Arts. A studio in Montmartre, in a park left in a state of charming neglect, on the *butte*, facing north. Neighbours from all round the world: Jorge, a Venezuelan painter; Vittorio, an Italian guitarist; Oliver, an American photographer; Nick, an English sculptor; Damian, a Romanian painter . . . something of a college campus, only older, more bohemian . . . tacked to the walls, notices, postcards and collages made by friends . . . two beds, side by side, in each place, property of the Cité, who also provide a desk, a chair, a stool, shelves, a hotplate and a fridge, the whole lot dating from the sixties and much the worse for wear.

On summer afternoons you can hang your washing outside, and get stung on the legs by the nettles. In the evening, walking between the buildings along the dark, paved alleyways of the park, you can see the artists' studios through their windows, high, brightly lit duplexes. There's a barbecue on the go, people sit around a table with a bottle of wine. Some neighbours arrive with more bottles, candles are lit. Cats dart around in the bushes, everyone's happy.

One day, after a night of discussion and argument with Oscar about money problems, I bumped into my upstairs neighbours on the doorstep. They have a little girl; he is getting on a bit, and they are still as poor as ever. She said to me: 'I think we are so lucky here. We can do what we like.'

It's not like him to ring so early. But he had been up all night working with Étienne, they never got to bed. He said he would be back this afternoon.

I wonder why I didn't answer. He may have thought that I wasn't at home, that I had slept elsewhere.

He had only been away three days, to that country house one hour from Paris where he and Étienne occasionally escape to write their first film. I love him, I don't want to hurt him.

But that morning even I ended up believing that I wasn't there.

I packed my travel bag, slipped on a sweater, a pair of shorts and my anorak. I went down to the street, got in the car and started driving, towards the south.

The sun quietly described its arc above the motorway. At first, I didn't think about anything. The plain rolled by, I listened to the radio.

By early afternoon I was beginning to regret not telling him I was going away, and was even regretting going away. At the first service station I stopped to phone him. I still had time to get back to Paris before evening. I would tell him that I had been seized by a whim, but now it had passed. He would be amused by that, he would understand what I didn't understand myself, he would reassure me. I felt very much in love, I was impatient to hear his voice.

I drove past the service station and parked in front of the restaurant. There was hardly anyone inside. I went straight to the telephone. There were three rings, then the click of the answerphone and his voice asking whoever it was to leave a message.

His voice. He must have come back then. He must have waited a bit, looked to see if I had left a message. No, that's what I would have done. He's not the worrying type. He must have said to himself that I'd gone swimming with Florence, or to an art gallery with Mary. And what about him, where had he gone off to?

He had changed the music on his answer-phone; it was a snatch of a theme tune from some television series, but I couldn't remember which one. After the beep I said nothing. I didn't hang up either, as if I were still waiting for him to answer. In the end I redialled, listened to him again, and once again said nothing.

I was hungry. I picked up a plate at the self-service café, filled it with everything I fancied, sat by the window and ate heartily. Then I went to get a coffee and drank it while smoking a cigarette.

Now I felt just fine. I had promised myself that I would phone him when I finished the meal, but it didn't seem so urgent now. In the end I didn't think about it any more. The thing that preoccupied me the most was not being able to remember where that music on the answerphone came from.

I drove back on to the motorway, still heading south, and I racked my brains again, running through all the television series I could think of, trying to remember their theme tunes. After all this time I realised that I couldn't even remember the one I had heard on the answerphone.

Towards the end of the afternoon, it started to rain. I was driving down the straight, deserted road through Les Landes, which I'd often travelled on and which I loved so much, bordered by an ocean of pine trees which stretch out on each side to infinity. When the first drops hit the windscreen I asked myself: does the rain start falling in the dimension of time or space? I ask myself this question every time I am driving and it starts raining, and every time I spin into a spiral of questions which never end in an answer.

At some point in the journey across Les Landes the hands of the dashboard clock started moving more and more slowly. At first I noticed nothing. Then they said the time on the radio and I realised that the clock was coming to a stop. Apparently there was a fault in the electrical circuit, no doubt due to the rain which must have seeped in everywhere.

I took the short cut which Oscar discovered, a small, winding country road, just in order to pass through Morlaas, just for the pleasure of seeing the cathedral again. The pleasure.

At Lourdes, the headlights began to dim, the windscreen wipers began to sweep more slowly, lifting a spray of water at each stroke.

At Lers, the first traces of snow began to appear by the roadside. It had stopped raining. I encouraged the car out loud, talking to it gently so that it wouldn't give up on me before we reached the cottage. I also prayed that I wouldn't encounter a policeman, with my almost defunct headlights. But the road was absolutely deserted, and fortunately I knew every bend by heart. I continued to climb. The radio had stopped working, but I thought it must be nearly midnight.

Finally I arrived at Éralitz. If the car packed up now I'd have no more than an hour's walk at most to get to the cottage. I felt relieved. The road continued to climb and, as always, my exaltation rose with it. Now I was almost at my mountain, my retreat.

At the exit from the village, which was fast asleep, the snow drifts rose up on each side of the small forest road. I wound down the window to breathe in the sharp, cold air. I parked in front of the refuge and got out of the car. The sky was white with stars.

There is a good quarter hour's walk through the snow. Then, on a hairpin bend, the forest gives way to a pale stretch of meadow, and there is the dark silhouette of the little stone house stuck on the side of the mountain, its roof covered with a blanket of white, like on a post-card. In the branches a night bird hoots, down in the valley the torrent roars, the snow crunches under my plimsolls and seeps inside, the pocket torch illuminates just enough to put one foot in front of the other, my bag feels heavy, the forest crackles, I get out of breath from the climb but I don't slow down, and there I am; with the shovel hanging from the roof I clear the entrance, the key in the lock makes a sharp click in the silence, the shutters grate a little as they swing heavily on their hinges, I push the door open and go in.

Start the meter, turn on the lights, the radiators, check everything is in place, downstairs and upstairs, that the mice haven't eaten the books, go back outside to clear the path a bit more in front of the house, get the ladder out to knock the pile of snow off the chimney, go back in, light a fire ... And sit in front of it with a steaming bowl of tea and a cigarette, feet now warm in a pair of walking boots, hours in front of the hearth, stoking and watching the fire.

In bed, since I couldn't get to sleep, I picked up a pen and some paper and, in spite of the cold, I wrote until dawn, until now, when I will finally go to sleep.

2

I've kept everything here, in my den. The few objects rescued from a dozen moves, photograph albums, love letters, children's drawings and poems, old cookery books, all sorts of books, even my school books, the Gaffiot, Greek grammars . . . I bought the cottage before I left France, and I left everything there, so as always to have a place to see my sons, Noé and Piero. Now it is myself I have come in search of.

I woke up in the early afternoon. It was snowing a bit, the mountain was magnificent. The Pic du Midi was invisible, submerged in a white mist, but the extraordinary indented ridge of the Ardiden was perfectly clear.

I called Oscar and once again got the answerphone. I said I was in Éralitz and hung up. I remained sitting on the bed, pensive, staring at the Pic du Midi, which was still invisible. The occasional, gently fluttering snowflakes formed a screen of softness beyond the windows.

It was strange. Since my departure, yesterday, my voice had disappeared from the answerphone, as if I had been immediately erased. Or as if I had never existed, in that other life, back there.

In the kitchen there remained a box of powdered milk, some semolina in a covered glass bowl and, in a coffee tin, some brown sugar scented by some opened vanilla pods. I made myself a milk pudding, which I ate warm.

I took a rucksack and went downstairs. The ski-lifts weren't in operation, and the refuge was closed. The ski season hadn't started yet. I tried everything, with and without the choke, I put oil and anti-freeze in the engine, but it was no use. The car refused to start. I went down to the village on foot, down the winding forest road. *The snow crunched beneath their feet*, wrote Piero in one of his 'novels'. Occasionally I heard the dark cawing of crows, a cracking beech twig.

The mechanic promised to come up and have a look at the car. I told him I had left the key in the ignition. The grocer's was closed, but the baker and the butcher were open, and I was able to buy enough to last until the next day. The butcher asked me if there was much snow up there, and whether I was staying for long. I also passed by the post office, to tell the postmaster I was there. If any letter arrives for me, he will keep it rather than forward it to Paris.

I have no idea how long I will be staying here, but I will have to wait at least until the car is repaired. The mechanic just phoned to say he came to fetch my battery and he would be recharging it overnight. He will have to come back to sort out the fan belt and the alternator.

When I got back to the house, after the long climb on foot from the village, all my muscles were warm, the blood flowed beneath my skin, I felt really good. I drank a large glass of water from the tap, delicious, ice-cold. The telephone rang just as I was in my bedroom, taking off my underpants to dry them out. It was Oscar. I slipped under the quilt and we talked for more than an hour.

Later, I watched the chart show on Canal +. On it was the Baschung video, *Madame Rêve*, where Fanny Ardent, at one point, bends down lovingly to tie his shoes. The image aroused me. I would have liked to be in her place. I would have taken the opportunity to kiss the ankles of the man, of Oscar.

In the beginning, I thought I was in love with him because he was young. A woman who loves a man younger than herself always asks herself questions. The idea persists that it is not very normal, that there is something a bit culpable about it. Especially if, on top of that, the man isn't making a decent living. In the heart of most women the fear of being possessed remains more than ever, and yet, deep down, so too does the inherited feeling that it is the man's job to pay. And often it is the gaze of other people which is the most difficult to bear. We live in a world so lacking in generosity.

Now I know that I love him because with him I have fun. A simple walk in town becomes a real party, the world is a universe overflowing with dreams to be realised, with him people and places are either extraordinary or infamous, but never unimportant, with him everything is funnier and larger than life, with him everything, everything is better.

From here, I can't see a soul, only the mountain. When it is not swallowed up in the mist. But usually the refuge is open, and I have friends there. In winter, when snowstorms cut me off, I know I can count on them. There are also the policemen who call by on skis to see if everything is all right.

That evening, it had stopped snowing. I went outside to look at the stars. Over the course of a night, and over the course of the seasons, the sky fluctuates and changes its face. After each stay in Paris, it gives me pleasure to see the signs of the passage of time, but the Pole Star stays fixed in its place, facing the door of my house, less bright than you sometimes imagine, but stubborn, at once a reference point and a pivot.

There were small lights on the summit of the Pic du Midi. They too must be looking at the sky. I dream about their life on duty up there, in the buildings of the observatory, when they are alone in the middle of the snow, with their domes which open on their telescopes pointed at the sky.

When he is here, Noé talks to me about the mysteries of the universe, he tells me what Stephen Hawking writes about quantum mechanics and relativity, and I am particularly interested in what he says about time, which is a variable dimension like any other, even if that is impossible to imagine. Noé says that science makes everything that is beautiful even more beautiful.

On the telephone I said to Oscar that I had started writing again. It wasn't premeditated, but I have the feeling that that is why I left. I told him I wanted to talk about our three years together. He is not afraid, he encourages me. I would like to write as one loves, like a toreador, that my novel should be a bullfight.

Writing this story is less exposing myself to the public than exposing myself a little more to Oscar. Words have such power. I remember the first hours of a former passion. In the middle of the night, I had gone to find D in his bed, to ask him to come to mine. In the morning, he had asked, 'Don't you have something to say to me?'

We both knew what it was I had to say to him. It was 'I love you'. But even though my whole person, all my actions and gestures cried out this truth, I somehow felt that those words would strip me bare, that by removing my final reserve they would leave me without protection, infinitely vulnerable. I knew that, once spoken, my love would become completely overwhelming, ineluctable, and I would never be able to escape it. And that's exactly what happened. For I resisted a moment, then I uttered the fatal words.

Just as, today, I write them.

3

I miss Oscar. I phone him frequently, during the day, at night. Yet he doesn't ask why I'm not coming back, now that the car is fixed. He understands. I worry about the telephone bill. Oscar tells me not to worry about anything, he'll find the money, he takes care of everything.

In any case, this old problem doesn't pre-occupy me so much here. All problems seem further away. I only go down to the village every two or three days, and if I get there too late to buy the newspaper, it's no big deal. In the evenings, instead of watching television or going out, I sit in front of the fire, or I consult my sky chart and observe the stars, which are like friends close at hand, since we belong to the same universe.

In the very beginning, when we aren't yet living together, I can be, from one day to the next, either madly in love or very detached. I have often since felt a nostalgia for that time when I could forget my passion so easily. One day, for example, he comes to see me when I am not expecting him. I am working, and I feel rather put out by his visit. I would prefer to carry on writing.

Other times, I can't resist kissing his feet fervently, as a sign of adoration. Since he doesn't like that at all, I mostly stop myself from doing it. It's funny how a fantasy which isn't shared can introduce humour into a lovers' situation, and at the same time exacerbate desire. Amused by the comical dimension of a misunderstanding, I feel just as vividly how a thwarted desire can become even more exciting.

Quite soon after meeting, each of us in our own way has to experience painful separations. One day during this very troubled period, at six o'clock in the morning, at the end of a sleepless night of arguments and tears, someone rings the doorbell as we are in the middle of making love.

It is Oscar's former girlfriend, who has escaped from the hospital where she is being treated for depression. He gets dressed quickly and goes downstairs. From the window I see them walk away slowly. He has his arm around her shoulder, she seems doped up on tranquillizers.

I wait for him, alone in the flat, for nearly two hours. I don't know what is going on, I am hypnotised by anxiety, the lack of sleep. When he comes back, looking pale and exhausted, he wants to make love to me straight away.

Around the same time, whenever I cry, he becomes violently angry, because he can't stand that, or else he has an urgent desire to make love to me.

Now we've finished with these games. I have little taste for pain, even if it sometimes makes the pleasure more bearable. At first you feel that pain exacerbates pleasure, but then you realise that it ends up by eating it away. I quickly returned to what I have always found more satisfying, a more joyful gluttony.

We first meet on a Friday, at seven o'clock in the evening. We are coming out of a postgraduate class at the literature faculty at Bordeaux. It must be November, because it is already dark and especially because I don't know anyone yet.

The students disperse into the car park and drive their cars back into town.

I am about to set off myself when one of them comes running up and asks if I can give him a lift. It is Oscar. I haven't noticed him before, and I don't feel anything in particular when I see him. I am not going his way, but I take him anyway as a favour.

After dropping him off, I must have been distracted, because I get lost trying to take a short cut. I drive for quite a while before I find the road home.

After that, we often sit together in the class, on Friday evenings and Saturday mornings. Every time I wear a dress he looks at my legs. I like looking at his chest and shoulders beneath his sweater. There are also his old, washed-out jeans, which he doesn't wear very often, because they have probably become a bit too tight for him, but which wonderfully show off his buttocks and his sex.

For a few months nothing happens between us except the odd exchange of looks and short, end-of-the-week conversations, probably soon forgotten on both sides. I say probably, because I have never thought to ask him how he felt about it, and I can't remember how I felt.

28

Towards the end of the academic year, we start seeing each other away from the university, and from then on things move quickly. I decide to live alone, with my sons, and I move house. It is summer, and the children have gone on holiday to their father's house, as they have done for a long time. I decide not to see Oscar any more, because it seems too difficult to love him, because my former lover is still around, because my emotional life is becoming too involved and painful. On his side it is even worse.

There are a number of break-ups and reconciliations I think, I can't remember very well, everything is so complicated and uncertain . . . Neither of us has ever cried so much. Yet there are also very happy days, I am happy in my new flat, with my new-found freedom, it is a beautiful autumn.

When we had both managed to leave our former lives and former loves, when he moved into my place, everything changed. We lived from day to day, carefree and pleasure-seeking. Our day never ended before four or five in the morning. When the children's started, around seven, I no longer saw them off, an hour later, with a goodbye kiss on the doorstep, as I had done for years. Noé, thirteen, and Piero, nine, got up by themselves, made their own breakfast, washed, dressed, put their satchels on their backs and set off, alone, each at his own time, each in his own direction. I was still asleep, exhausted from love.

Once, when I got up, I cried out. At a time when I thought the flat was empty, Piero came to meet me in the corridor. He too was afraid, on hearing me cry out. He hadn't woken up in time, and had stayed in his room, making up complicated stories with his Lego, without turning on his radio-cassette player, taking care not to make his sounds and his voices too loud. He had a sheepish look on his face, because he had missed school and because he had given me a fright. We went to get a bite to eat at the McDonalds down the street, I apologised to him and he went to school in the afternoon. That evening, for once, I went to meet him at the end of school.

By the start of the next school year, Oscar and I had left France, and the children went to live with their father.

When I recall the few months we lived together

in Bordeaux, I can see the sunlight flooding into the flat, evenings at the local pub, a picnic by the Garonne with some of Oscar's friends . . .

Then, towards the end, my first nights in the cottage, with Noé and Piero, and also Julien, my brother, and José, who were there to do some work on the place. We slept up in the hay loft. We could get water up through the tap, but the electricity wasn't connected yet. Down below, a trench cut across the room. Julien and José must have pulled out the huge rocks, which were stuck in the ground like icebergs, to redo the floor. All the large stones were subsequently piled up in front of the house and were like a new mountain which we climbed up to bask in the sun.

We had to go far away. Oscar had given up on his idea of doing his thesis at the university of Baton Rouge, in Louisiana. He already had a mind to launching himself in the cinema. Somewhat at random, but probably because of the prospect of wide, virgin spaces, we flew to Montreal.

4

On our arrival at Mirabel we walked softly down the long airport corridor. We didn't yet know where we were going. Once we reached the exit, we stopped to discuss it. Oscar went off in search of an information desk, and I sat down by the window, next to a trolley stacked higher than a car full of immigrants on a road in the south-west of France.

A few weeks earlier, I had phoned my editor in Montreal to let him know of my decision to come and stay in Quebec. Oscar, who thinks everyone is as welcoming and generous as he is, said, you'll see, he'll receive you like a queen. But the news hadn't got my editor jumping for joy. He had merely warned me that it wasn't easy to come and live here.

Oscar returned with some brochures, and we chose a cheap hotel on Saint-Hubert. From our taxi we watched the vast, flat landscape roll past, still basking in the gentle last days of a marvellous Indian summer, the trees turning every shade of red.

The hotel, which was opposite the bus station, was run by Hindus who spoke English, much to Oscar's delight, who seized every occasion to practise his accent with the excitement of a child with a toy. We got our cases up to the shabby room in three stages, then we had a shower and went out.

It was around four or five o'clock in the afternoon, it was cold and already grey. We had celebrated the night before in Paris, our bodies were feeling the effects of a sleepless night followed by a twelve-hour journey, including an eight-hour flight in a noisy, decrepit charter plane with no movie, and six hours' worth of jet lag.

It seemed like we were the only ones to notice the cold. People were walking round in shirtsleeves on this bleak Sunday, in the gloomy streets and the empty spaces of the east-central part of town, under a colourless sky, and everything seemed perfectly normal to them.

We went back into the centre and sat down in a Howard Johnson, on Saint-Catherine, with a quarter chicken and two large glasses of water filled with ice. I could see that Oscar was so disappointed by his first view of the city that he was close to tears. He had dreamed so much about departing, and for so long. And now that he had done it, it was like waking up.

During the following days we wandered around the city for hours, shivering alternately with the cold and with fever. We had both caught violent colds, which we treated with equally violent medication, which can be bought like sweets from any grocer's shop. We had now moved into a small, slightly more comfortable hotel on Saint-Denis, near to the Square Saint-Louis in the middle of the student quarter. We were in a daze because of the pills, and we walked several kilometres on foot from east to west and from north to south, down long, straight streets, like feverish ghosts, looking for a flat in a nice part of town.

Finally we found a two-room flat on the fourth and top floor of a block in the rue Aylmer, a charming street with smart houses, near to the American-style town centre.

An autumn evening in Montreal. Oscar stretched out on the carpet, me lying on the couch with my legs in the air against the wall, admiring the lace on my stockings. The rain has stopped, I think, but as I look outside I see the drops running down the window-pane, not new drops, but the ones from before, which have been hanging there. Why are they starting to run? Perhaps it is the wind, or it has started raining again. He is still watching TV, zapping like a madman between the thirty-two channels, there's *Mad Max* in English, he says, look, I glance at the screen and then turn back to the outside, to the night, with the reflection of the round lamp, the drops dripping and the lights in the windows of some of the flats opposite, then nothing else, it must be late, three or four in the morning perhaps, we always stay up until the night is so far advanced that it seems that nothing exists any more.

I sometimes wonder whether there might be a voyeur over there with his binoculars, watching us when we are making love, or just doing nothing. Everything which goes on behind these dozens of windows... I have already observed the neighbour in the building opposite, just below us, he is a student, he has a table with a few sparse papers and a little Canadian flag, the red maple leaf. In order to see him I have to go out on to the balcony, but he isn't there very often, and when he is, he doesn't do anything. He sits next to the table in an armchair, picks up a book and reads, has the vague air of someone reading. Even though he is not a great subject for observation, I start imagining his life. I wouldn't want us to be observed, Oscar and me, I always check to make sure we can't be seen, but on the other hand I say to myself that anyone watching us would have a better show than that offered by my neighbour.

For the moment, the mirrors here still reflect only ourselves.

Every time that, from the window of the flat, I saw one of those yellow school buses passing along the rue Aylmer down below or, even worse, a little child with a satchel on his back, I thought about my sons, about the time when they were near me, when I took them to school each day and went to pick them up. And I cried.

The misfortune of women and men is that they are obliged to choose, that they must leave one road to take another. But it's a much bigger misfortune to have no choice at all, or not to give yourself one.

If I suffered from being separated from my sons, it was at least as much because I found myself suddenly deprived of their support as through the fear of missing them.

I suffered because I didn't regret it. I was free, I was living the life I wanted to live.

Oscar writes screenplays, has meetings with writers and producers. After a collaboration with a trendy magazine, I write regularly for a serious daily paper. A few book reviews, but mainly a weekly column, where I am asked to give a foreigner's point of view on Quebec. 'Don't pull any punches,' they specified. Thanks to which, every week, I receive a torrent of insults on the letters page.

During this winter in Montreal we experience at first hand what it means to be an immigrant.

Our best, most wonderful friend is Windsor. A writer, he lives in Miami, but makes long and frequent visits to Montreal, where he presents a television programme. He introduced us to his numerous friends, Haitians like himself, and I fell in love with one of them, L.

It is an impossible love, for a whole host of

reasons, and in the first place because I don't
want to risk losing Oscar. Then, if that's not
enough to convince me, I tell myself that some
loves are more beautiful, more disturbing and
longer lasting when they remain impossible.

Sometimes we go dancing at the Keur Samba,
a Caribbean nightclub where we meet our
friends. One evening, sitting side by side at the
bar, L and I hold hands, for a long time, and
carried on talking to our group as if nothing
were happening.

I'm very afraid that Oscar will notice, not
because I dread his reaction (I know that he
would pretend he hadn't seen anything), but for
fear of hurting him. Yet this hand in mine
makes me feel so happy that I can't bring
myself to let go. There is something desperate
about it, an emotion perhaps similar to how
you might feel just before dying, when you can
taste keenly the last moments of your life and
you regret it infinitely. Sometimes I think it is
perhaps solely for that emotion that I loved L,
while loving Oscar is taking on life hand-to
hand.

That evening, we stay on till the club closes,
dancing the beguine pressed tight together. At
the end of the night everyone is totally merry.

We start reading each other's palms. Oscar flirts
a little with a very pretty Haitian woman. Since
I want to match his standards of discretion, I
make out not to be watching them.

The rose-dark of the first days of
snowstorms . . . The fresh blanket of snow, still
virgin and shining bright, is reflected in the sky,
which remains pink and luminous all night.

I watched the weather channel, Météomédia,
looking for record cold temperatures. Windsor
makes fun of me, calls me Miss Météo.

One evening, when the temperature reaches
−32°, Oscar says, I have to see this. He takes
off his sweater and T-shirt, opens the door and
goes out onto the balcony. Bare-chested, facing
the thousand lights of the tower blocks hanging
in the night, he leaps into the snow, his arms
raised in a victory sign.

In spite of temperatures of between −20 and −30
degrees some evenings, and even sometimes
during the day, I refuse to go out in boots and
trousers. I put on a small dress, suspenders,
sheer stockings, high-heeled shoes. As my coat
only reaches my knees, as soon as I go down

into the street my legs are gripped in a frozen vice. I take Oscar's arm, so as not to slip on the ice, until we reach the taxi rank.

Since I have been beautiful for the whole evening, Oscar, when we get back, is that much more eager. We sometimes make love with so much rage that we appear to be raping each other.

There are some very intimate things which I can't write. To write them would be to condemn them to death. Certain rituals of tenderness, for example, certain laughs, certain sexual practices. As long as these things remain unwritten, we can relive them a thousand times without the feeling of repeating ourselves. Often they are so small, so fragile. To speak them would be to ruin them, to repeat them having spoken them would be to copy ourselves. Contrary to what we like to believe in our chat-show world, the word can easily become a thief of life, identity and freedom.

The ink that flows from me, offered up . . . Even for the most misanthropic person, to write is to love. The person who writes the best is the one who loves the best. You will never find a

43

better expression of human love than in a book
by Céline.

Sometimes, when I feel overcome by an
exhaustion close to that which follows love, I
think that this ink which has spilled out tends
to transform me into a peculiar kind of vampire
who, not content with drinking the blood of
others, feeds herself with her own blood. Thrill-
ing life.

At the end of the winter, one night, I stand in
the living-room contemplating the town.
Through the window, tower blocks, buildings
of all sizes, punctuated by windows still lit
up, in the distance the green neon sign of the
Holiday Inn, and the vast sky, grey banks of
cloud fused into the dark, with storm clouds
reeling off in front like smoke.

Three in the morning, silence. Beyond the
concrete blocks, the north, vast, cold, deserted
spaces. Montreal, a large, modern city at the
gates of nothingness. The mixed feelings I have
had for this country since I arrived (bewilder-
ment and exaltation, then disillusionment)
change that night into a single feeling, more
peaceful, sadder and more beautiful than all the

others: sympathy, in the strongest sense of the term.

That night, looking at the city frozen in silence and cold, I feel that the sleeping consciousness of millions of people, an amalgam of different races, relinquishing the vindictive energy of the day, of the constant struggle of every day, I feel that this sleeping consciousness leaves souls bare, finally allows the truth of man, the grandeur and misery of human ambitions to appear.

And I think that these six months in this snow-covered city have been like my wedding dress, the dress of a ceremony full of slowness, beyond which lurks an adventure which is both troubling and exciting. When Oscar came to live with me in Bordeaux, it still had something provisional about it. But when we left everything in our former lives to come to Montreal, when we chose to live there together, in the same flat, like two shipwrecked souls on a desert island who decide to share the same cave, for reasons of survival, then I felt we were two new persons, two strangers almost, and that we were really on the road now, to a destination which remained unknown.

And that evening, at the end of that winter

where we are trapped in the virgin expanses of snow, face to face with one another, I understand that the ceremony is reaching its conclusion, and that beyond our isolation, our crises of doubt and our transports of passion, we have touched the truth of each other, in its nakedness, and must now depart on a journey to continue our exploration, like you do after the wedding.

On the first day of spring, when the sun in one go melted the last of the snowdrifts, the streets and the terraces of the cafés filled with people. On the roof of the building opposite a white-haired man in dark glasses, a yellow sweater and blue trousers started playing a violin, sitting on a folding stool.

And we decided to set off for the United States.

5

We have our biggest row in the wild city of New York. One night, at the Chelsea Hotel, a very long discussion on poverty and immigration, during which we express slightly differing points of view, turns into a personal quarrel.

It's always the same. Behind the idea is the man. And a battle of ideas can quickly give way to a conflict of two personalities.

In the middle of the night, then, the discussion turns into a drama. It's the first leg of our journey, and we are questioning the whole of our relationship. In the end, Oscar packs his bags. It's all over. I am already beginning to think about what I will do tomorrow, whether I will continue the journey, alone.

And then, I don't know how, everything sorts itself out, and we end up going to sleep together. It must be nearly dawn.

We argue frequently during the course of these three months, it seems to me. I remember one time; I am driving, in a desert landscape – it must have been Nevada – we wind each other up so much that he gets out of the car with his bag, and I drive on, alone, well shot of him.

A few kilometres later I turn round, hoping with all my heart that I will find him again. On that occasion, the argument centred on a bar of chocolate.

Coming into Miami, we crash the car which we bought in Montreal. It is dark, Oscar has been driving for a long time. That morning, we had stopped to go bathing on Daytona Beach. The warmth and beauty of the day in our bodies. One second of lapsed concentration and, taking a left turn, we hit the car coming in the opposite direction at full speed. The windscreen shatters and steam comes pouring out of the engine.

Neither of us is injured. I get out of the car.

I have hardly set my foot down when a tall guy in a uniform, a Gary Cooper type, puts his hand on my shoulder and asks me if everything is all right, calling me darling and showing me his detective's badge. Am I in some sort of film?

The detective speaks into his mobile, the driver of the other car slumps on his bonnet, our lovely Oldsmobile is completely stove in, a write-off.

A couple of minutes later, we are surrounded by police cars. Their lights are flashing all over. They extract our luggage from our car *in extremis*, so that the pick-up truck, which has also appeared on the scene already, can take it away without further ado to the breaker's yard, while Gary Cooper bundles us into a taxi and leaves us his card. Goddamn, I wish he would call me darling again, concern himself a bit more with my state of health. But everything is sorted out before you can blink. It must be what's known as American efficiency.

Thereupon, our taxi loses itself in the streets of Miami, and that's how we arrive at Windsor's, hours late, when everyone is already asleep. He greets us with his usual broad smile, and we sit out behind the house to chat while sipping drinks beside the pool, accompanied by a large toad who is taking the air.

Lake, beach, whistling bird, palm trees, flame trees, trees with purple flowers, trees growing in a spiral, with white roots rolled around their trunks and splayed out wide into the rough grass, warm wind in the trees, sky everywhere. Miami, in the heart of town.

Woken this morning by Windsor tapping on his typewriter. Windsor's talent. The clicketty-clack of the typewriter counts out spasmodic time, with flashes and silences, deconstructs the metronomic time of the clock.

Alone in a wooden hut at the edge of the beach, all around the green space the houses of men, and still the wind, the pages of my note-book flutter, why write this journal, my jour-nal? I don't think I have ever done this in my life, except when I was a child, when life was raw, playing football in the street with the boys, riding a bike which was too small or much too big, as if time were immobile, living like a young animal, without a past, without a tomorrow . . .

The unpainted wooden fence, the soft green bush with its large yellow flowers are reflected in the turquoise water of the pool, where the occasional drop of rain forms concentric circles. Always the warm wind on our skin, it is nearly evening, at five o'clock we had our only meal of the day, fried bananas, grits, avocado salad, rice, mushroom sauce, cake, orange juice served in tall glasses filled with ice, coffee, cigarette, we chatted a while on the terrace, next to the pool, and Windsor is back at his table, tapping away, we can hear from here the almost uninterrupted sound of his typewriter . . .

I have a need to look at the water, to feel the wind, my head is like an air current, crossed by lights, sensations, vertiginous stairways, it is like the leaves of the big trees swaying in the wind, you can't tell whether it is happiness or despair, a sort of pleasure in being absent from yourself, the flow of the world, eyes wide open to let everything in, an eagerness in your breast, and writing as a means of keeping a hold, or perhaps of entering more fully into the illusion.

Drops fall on the notebook. It would be more intimate if I could give the reader these stains of diluted ink.

Waukeenah, Florida. I am sitting in the doorway of an old-fashioned motel, run by an old Vietnamese couple, not far from Tallahassee. The rain falls on the pines, the palm trees, the tarmac, the rented white Chrysler parked in front of the room. A heavy, dense, warm rain, like we had all week in Miami. Oscar is still sleeping.

I look at the landscape, the Baron convertible. I like cars.

I go back into the room and take three photos.

First from the back of the room, Oscar asleep, the sheet pulled back over his buttocks, with, in the background, the open door, through which can be seen the car and the rain.

Then from the doorway, the trees and the road in the rain.

Finally, at pavement level, the wet grass and concrete.

In the middle of a road in Louisiana, a tortoise. Oscar avoids it, then comes back to take it off the road, where it is in danger of being crushed. He parks at the entrance to a field, gets out, catches the tortoise . . . which sprays a long, powerful stream of piss all down his legs. He puts it down by the roadside, in the grass, safe from danger, and, to teach it some manners, undoes his flies and pisses on it in turn.

In Texas, Oscar slows down, addresses the cows beside the road in a loud voice, with the

WHEN YOU LOVE YOU MUST DEPART

expressions and the accent of a peasant from the Gers. The cows interrupt their chewing to listen to him.

I give him a blow-job as we drive along the deserted Route 291, in the direction of El Dorado. With one hand I hold my hat on my head.

The pleasures of a convertible, sky right into the car and fresh air against the skin. On each side of the road prairie as far as the eye can see, trees, cacti, brown cows, now and again, rarely, wooden signs announcing a ranch. One of them is called *High Lonesome*.

Later on, grandiose deserts, cliffs and arid hills, dotted with tufts of grass. Dinner in Iraan, cowboy country, a broad main street, a few shacks on each side, dusty and ruined. One restaurant, where we are the only customers. Local steaks, a very tender meat with a pronounced taste, accentuated by slices of onion and green pepper.

Another time, in Arkansas, same love scene on the move, with the hood down, but at night, in stormy weather, beneath a black sky striped with flashes of lightning.

Mountains stretching to infinity, superimposing their lines on the blue mist, canyons, volcanos, rock arches, forests of cacti, red boulders, white boulders, fields of black larva, hard sun, immeasurable horizons, deserts of sand or pebbles, interrupted only by the ribbon of tarmac being swallowed up by the car . . .

And the cities, New Orleans, happy town, San Francisco, fun town, Las Vegas, electric town, Salt Lake City, counting-house town, El Paso, turnpike town, Tombstone, ghost town . . .

And the old couple in a bar in Plattsburgh, the only audience of a rock group screaming into their microphones on a tiny stage,

and the Amish on their carts in the smell of cut grass,

and the thousand lights of a factory, at night, in the clammy stench of Georgia,

and the huge bed at the Prytania Inn in New Orleans,

and Lucie Brind'amour in Baton Rouge, Hunt in Austin, Warren and Marie in Boulder, Mary and George in New York,

and the Indian from India watching his cricket match on television in Socorro,

and my first real encounter with an Ameri-

can Indian, in the Navajo territory, by the side
of a small road, in a flaming red sunset, this
Indian with his pigtail down his back and the
traditional policeman's uniform, who stopped
me for speeding,

and the great barefoot jumps in the white
powder of White Sands,

and the old man who told us his life story in
the first bar after the exit from Death Valley,

and the waitress with the serious voice in a
Spanish restaurant in Tucson,

and the moment when the one-armed bandit
in Las Vegas spat out a never-ending stream of
coins,

and in the South, the little black girls with
brightly coloured ties in their hair,

and the torrential rain in the bayou of Atch-
afalaya,

and the ubiquitous *We Support Our Troops*
signs,

and the guy with his dog, wearing sunglasses,
at midnight in Greenwich Village,

and the smell of honeysuckle in Central
Park,

and on the pavement, a homeless person
sleeping on a plastic bag bearing the inscription
I Love New York,

and the tiny, enclosed garden where they have reproduced the flora that would still exist on Manhattan if they hadn't built the city,

and the fragment of old Indian pottery discovered and offered to us by a couple of archaeologists somewhere in the Rockies,

and the dark eyes of the Indian children,

and the man from Bordeaux with the head of a boxer on a Greyhound bus,

and the picnic tables at the foot of the monument to Geronimo,

and the black man playing guitar beneath a leaden sun in a small alleyway in the mining town of Bisbee,

and the heat, the light and the vast skies,

and the hundred-carriage train passing through a ghost town,

and the mud devil I made in the furnace of Death Valley . . .

Road, motels, road, whichever of us wasn't driving stretched out in the convertible, ate the blue-white or starry sky with their eyes, ate the wind, or sat on the hood, at the back, their feet on the seat, dominating the road, splitting the landscape, intoxicated with life.

6

As long as I can remember, I have always written to express my love. In my notebooks – of which only half remain, since at the age of seventeen I burned all those from the preceding years; in my letters; all my short texts; my novels ... to the point where I no longer know clearly whether I write in order to love better, or whether I love in order to write better.

Even during quite short flings, I have always had a feeling of being in love, if only a fleeting or secret one. Oscar says it is the same for him. Since the start it has been obvious, for him as for me, that we have both held on to our freedom. But it is not so easy also to love elsewhere. Of course, there is the fear of Aids, which is understandable and quite real, but it is often convenient to hide behind that fear other equally understandable fears, like that of losing a love. A little less easy to admit, and much more difficult to protect yourself against.

Faced with a man who attracts me, I am sometimes cursed with still being able to act like a little girl, as if it were the first time, the real first time, overwhelmed with a mixture of fear and boldness, terminally stupid. Yet is it not precisely because of this miracle that we like to be seized by the feeling of love, because of this fragility it throws us into, consigning all experience to forgetfulness and uselessness, exposing us to the world in our misery and nakedness, with only our desire as a weapon of survival?

It's strange, when I think of those who have loved before me, it is mainly men who come to mind. Nerval, Verlaine, Schwob. Kafka. I feel I understand them so well. Because I feel tenderness for the first ones, and because I am in love with Kafka. Do you really understand better the ones you love?

What I am is all women, because we are all lovers, the Cretan *Parisienne* leaping between the horns of bulls, Ariadne giving her thread to Theseus, then, abandoned by him, scouring the

countryside with Dionysus, Nausicaa playing
ball and finding Ulysses naked on a beach,
Sappho entirely devoted to love and poetry,
Phaedra in love with her son-in-law against the
social laws, Antigone standing before the Law
on her brother's behalf, Melusine, woman-
spirit-serpent, and also the wife of Bluebeard
slipping the key into the forbidden door, Little
Red Riding Hood skipping through the forest
to meet the wolf, and Ondine in the streams
crying for her wandering knight, Emma intoxicated with Rodolphe, I am all these women
except Penelope, all these women in turn
impatient, elusive, indomitable, tragic or
comic, hedonistic, fragile but stronger than
fragile, adventurous, free.

And what I want is love, careless love and
love which questions everything, love which
brings rebirth, passion-love, love from afar, *fin
amor*, love which makes you go beyond yourself, platonic love, sexual love, weightless love,
dark love, light love, tenderness-love, faithful
love, unfaithful love, jealous love, generous
love, free love, dream love, adoration-love,
mystical love, instinct-love, the love you make,
the before, during and after of love, love which
burns, modest love, secret love, shouted love,

love which is an ache in the stomach, love which warms the stomach, love which paralyses and love which gives wings, love to death, love to life, first love, lost love, wounded love, the next love, because there is no model, because you must invent your loves, invent your life.

Dreams, networks of memory . . . journeys . . . pleasures . . . All together, all mixed up . . . I write this in my bed, as always my fingers are covered with ink . . . I love that, I love that.

That summer we come back to Éralitz. Everything is exactly as we left it, after moving in. Books, linen and crockery in boxes, dismantled furniture.

The mountain is magnificent.

The day the electricity company come to start the meter, at the edge of the forest, and we succeed, by joining up all the extension cables we possess, in setting up a temporary lamp outside the kitchen window (another metre of cord and we'd have got it inside), the moment seems as extraordinary to us as a biblical *fiat lux*.

And then there was light, even if only from

outside the house, a little lamp hanging in the dark with moths flitting around it.

There was a lerot which often wandered along the rafters when we were sitting in front of the fire in the evening. A lovely little white animal, with black rings round its eyes like a mask. We also had a dormouse, which clambered over the bedroom wall, with its adorable fur like a grey squirrel. And also some field mice, sociable, slightly shy little creatures, who willingly came to do their shopping in the kitchen.

Unfortunately, after a year, all these friendly rodents began to take over the place and, in desperation, I had to steel myself to poison them.

That summer we work on the cottage, with my brother Julien. There are often people around. The children are there.

It is the first time I have really made contact again with my brother, who was with me throughout my childhood and adolescence. It has become too difficult to keep track of him and his mad schemes. When Julien throws himself into something, he does it whole-heartedly. Fortunately, he has a strong instinct for freedom which always saves him. So he switches to some other craze. His current one is Africa.

As Piero is always playing soldiers, using the lie of the land, the trees and rocks, which probably take on mythical dimensions in his imagination, Oscar nicknames him General Schwarzkopf. He and Julien only ever call him by this name. Piero is always in a good mood. He and I go collecting branches in the forest, and Noé chops them with the axe.

In the morning, before we start work, Julien wanders off a way into the forest to play his djembé. As he is about to go on tour with his group he needs to carry on rehearsing. He goes out there again at nightfall.

Later I learn that they could hear the beat of African drums as far away as the other side of the valley, something of a surprise to peasants and tourists alike.

In the forest, we play music, we build huts, we have fun, we dream we are alone. We also go to find wood, for the fire, and mushrooms, for omelettes. We do everything in the forest. Even make love, of course.

In the early days, as we don't have any hot water yet, we fill some bottles with cold water and take showers with them, stark naked on the grass of the meadow, in the morning sun.

Gradually the house takes shape. I put the shelves back up, set out my books. I begin to give a personal touch to the small rooms under the roof: a Babar poster in the west room, a dressing table in mine . . .

Towards the end of August, the cows begin coming down into the meadow. We see their large heads through the window when we wake up or, in the evening, their pale, ample forms moving slowly in the dark. Like buddhas.

The cottage isn't big, but it is big enough to entertain lots of friends. It is one of those houses which are inhabited by happiness, like the one I knew before, next to a lake, or the ones I lived in, a long time ago, next to the ocean.

In mid-September we leave for Paris. The flat

we have rented, in the rue Véron, between Montmartre and Pigalle, is empty. A few cases, a mattress, that's all. There isn't even a telephone, the electricity is cut off, we have to wait four or five days for it.

In the street, transvestites ply their trade night and day. The first evening, as we don't have any light inside, we sit at the window watching them, them and their clients. One of them is a fair resemblance of a woman, with his silicone breasts which he never tires of admiring, but the others . . . they are so strapping . . .

The whole time that we live there, I continue to love watching them. It is always strange, sometimes very poetic, or very sad, and sometimes also dead funny. In my mind I call them 'the angels'. When I talk about them I refer to them both as 'he' and 'she', without being able to make up my mind.

There is one who always stands next to the church, directly under the NO ENTRY sign and beneath the inscription NO BILL STICKERS painted on the wall. He braves all these interdictions with perfect peace of mind. He is tall and stocky, but has a regal poise and is very

graceful. His hair tied back, always well coif-
fured, and tastefully made up.

In winter, perched on his stiletto heels, he
wears a long fur coat. When finally a client
presents himself (in the end I am able to ident-
ify as well as he the most likely potential
clients among the passers-by), his pink lips
open in a charming smile and, his head tilted
in an almost maternal gesture, his gaze direct,
he quickly opens the flaps of his coat to reveal
his flesh neatly corseted in a white basque.
When he gets bored, he lights a cigarette and
then coughs a bit.

As we are at the window, and it is dark inside
the flat, our neighbour calls across to offer us
a candle. He brings it to us and we become
friends.

During the autumn we talk to each other,
window to window, from one side of the street
to the other. Sometimes, other neighbours join
in the conversation. Franck lives in a studio
fifteen metres square, he is a musician, brim-
ming over with plans which are far from easy
to realise, even though he is talented and
ready to move heaven and earth. And all these
words, all these plans exchanged over the street

help us all to disguise our anxieties about the future. He spends the greater part of the day on the phone, walking up and down in front of his single window. Otherwise he composes and plays, and he can be seen standing, wielding his drumsticks with brio above his large marimba installed beneath the mezzanine floor.

Our financial problems had got a lot worse. Unable to pay the rent any longer, we finally had to give up the flat. And I didn't have a publisher any more.

Oscar began working on a feature film with Étienne, a project which they believed in a lot. I encouraged him to pursue it. I wrote my novel and found a new publisher.

We spent a large part of the winter and spring in Éralitz, where we could work and go skiing or walking with friends.

Sometimes I so adore life. But sometimes too I am tired, and I think I could gladly die there and then, my life is so full.

7

When I was an adolescent, I was afraid I wouldn't know how to go about things, in order to live, once I had entered the adult world. And then I arrived there without realising it, and everything happened of its own accord, I have never been afraid of anything since.

I was nineteen, I was pregnant. Yannick was doing his military service, and I lived on my own, in a lonely old house next to the ocean.

At that time and in that place I had neither neighbours nor friends, but I didn't suffer from loneliness at all. I didn't have a telephone or a television either. There was just one stove to heat the whole house. Also, on winter evenings, it was a bit cold. I got into my big metal bed, switched on the radio and knitted little things for my baby – things so tiny they could never fit any baby, only my sisters' dolls. Or else I read.

When Yannick had leave, for a weekend, we would go to bed and stay there for two days, making love non-stop. I was perfectly happy.

One day, Prunelle, the cat, who was also pregnant – and was due the same day as me, what's more – climbed on to the roof of a neighbouring villa. But with her fat belly she was no longer as agile. She couldn't get down. I heard her miaowing wretchedly, so I went to her rescue.

It was the end of March, and the house Prunelle had ventured into was a holiday home, like all the villas round about. There wasn't a living soul for hundreds of metres on each side. The weather was fine, the warm air smelt of the sea, the sand, the mimosa and the pine needles. I was just as handicapped as Prunelle, but I climbed the gate. In a shed behind the villa I found a ladder. I leaned it against the wall, and went to fetch the cat.

Before my baby was born, I had cut out of a sheet of cardboard twenty or so announcement cards, which I had decorated with individual drawings in green ink. The life which I had rather dreaded a few years earlier was turning out to be full of wonders, an afternoon of drawing, a walk by the sea, reverie in the sun, a night of reading, writing a love letter or a poem . . .

Deep down I have never lost this enthusiastic surprise at the richness of life. But I am probably less serene nowadays. Once again, as when I was an adolescent, fear lurks within me. Did I already have this feeling of loss which I sometimes feel so strongly today? Perhaps. Apart from a few elements, I have so few memories of my past life. My whole memory consists of a few sensations.

When he was small, Piero sometimes asked me, 'Do you love Yannick?' I would answer something like, 'Yes, but it's not like it was before,' and he would insist, 'You must love him, he's your husband.' Yannick and I had separated when Piero was just one, and I felt that he had never had to suffer because of it, unlike Noé, who was bigger.

And yet he too was experiencing nostalgia, nostalgia for that short period when he had experienced us being together. How else can one explain such a desire to see me conform to a law, to a morality, that no one had taught him?

Each time I was pregnant, I felt full of happiness to the tips of my fingers, vibrant with life and sure of myself. Even when my stomach grew bigger, it didn't kill my sexual appetite, quite the opposite. In the street I looked men straight in the eye. I felt beautiful.

The second time, I also became religious. Until then I had had no other gods than those of Olympus who, in my imagination, really inhabited the world. Now I was discovering the Bible, the Gospels, and above all the Apocalypse, which I read and reread. I had moments of mysticism, like blinding flashes, which I called 'orgasms of the soul', since it seemed the most appropriate term. During the day I had nothing to do except go for walks, go and see the sea and read. I savoured each action, each moment.

As an adolescent I devoured books, often several a day, in class, in the refectory, in the dormitory, lining up, anywhere. I wanted to be true to Rimbaud and Nietzsche, I adored Nerval, Artaud, Roussel, Daumal, Jerry Rubin, I could recite by heart whole pages of *Paroles*, of *Ondine*, of *The Odyssey* in Greek, or *The Metamorphoses* in Latin.

How far back do I need to go to find the rupture? The childhood years? As I said, I was a young animal. Spontaneous, coquettish, proud, quarrelsome. Perhaps there is no other rupture than the nostalgia for that state. No other rupture than the infinite succession of tears imposed by the passage of time, the succession of all those lives, all those loves, all those beings, all those places, all those books, all those selves, abandoned and lost forever . . . No other rupture than that of all those departures, past and future, for once you have started to leave, who would want to stop?

What is more distressing than the end of *Citizen Kane*, when we learn that the hero, Charles Foster Kane, has always lived with this rift in his heart, the regret for the sledge of his childhood in the snow, which bore the inscription *Rosebud*? Rosebud was also the name given by Orson Welles to the clitoris of his girlfriend. Is this pink button not the very image of that little pure being which we have probably never been, but which we continue to hanker for all our lives? I would like my novel to be like that film, a life like a ring around a regret, but I can't give a name to what it is I have lost.

So I start evoking past happinesses, as if those

of today weren't enough, as if I were becoming more and more voracious, as if I feared that life is escaping me, already.

Oscar sometimes says that if we split up one day, we would need to go on seeing one another, in order to make love. Normally, when he says that, I reply that I don't really think so, that to my mind, once something is over, it is over on every level. But on other occasions I say nothing, I don't know what to think, and that makes me sad.

This afternoon, on my own, I put on some cassettes, Midnight Oil, Rita Mitsouko, Nirvana, Prince, at full blast, and I danced and sang.

Tonight, Oscar and I spoke for more than two hours on the phone. Once everything was simple, nothing frightened me. And now I am starting to reflect, hesitate, think about protecting myself, everything is becoming complicated. Now I have become a woman of my time, for whom the most natural gestures are the most problematic.

I refuse to enter that world where you must renounce chance, risk, adventure. I don't like to think that making a baby presupposes a mature decision, a calculation, a rational choice. I don't like to think that I could become rational. I want to go on feeling that my life is at once precious and ridiculous, I want to remain light, fragile and hardy like a wild flower, one of those red poppies which flourish next to cemeteries and railway lines.

8

I left Éralitz this morning. It is exactly eight days since I arrived. I left the car in the village, it is too clapped out to make the return journey. I caught a bus to Lourdes, and now find myself on the high-speed train. Luckily, there is no one sitting next to me, I can write in peace.

Normally, I prefer to read or look out of the window. Once, when I was returning to Bordeaux after my first interview with my first future publisher, there was a magnificent rainbow, which stood over the landscape for the whole journey, that is, a few hours and five hundred kilometres.

Yesterday, I tidied and cleaned the whole house. I threw out the ashes from the fire and any food that might go off, but I forgot to throw out the bread. I realised when I was on the bus, but it was too late. It will attract mice, and since I also forgot to put down any poison, once the bread runs out they might start to eat my books.

It really is a house for me. A house where I can't stay more than a few weeks in a row, a house where my memories are in danger of being eaten when I am away. It's exactly what I need.

In less than two weeks, we will have to leave Paris. The accommodation at the Cité des Arts is only allocated on a temporary basis, and we will not be in a position to take another flat.

I have often dreamed of living in a hotel. A hotel means that you can leave at any moment, that you are not encumbered with things, nor with shopping, cooking and all the other onerous household chores, it means that you feel like going out every evening, that you can stay locked away for days if the fancy takes you, if it's a large hotel, you can order up champagne and fruit in the middle of the night, if it's a small hotel, you have your morning coffee in the nearest bar... Or else live in a circus, always on the road... A nomad, that's what I would have liked to be. They have been eliminated, but one day, you'll see, the nomads will repopulate the world. Once, in a letter, L called me 'my gipsy'. It's the nicest thing anyone has ever said to me.

In less than two months, we will return to Éralitz, we will be happy there for a few weeks, and then we will want to move on. I don't know what will happen then, and I like not knowing.

Sometimes I think that, in some ways, I was freer when I was poor. If I needed money, I would look for a job as a waitress, for example, that didn't pose any problems. Today, not only would I be afraid of being recognised by a reader if I became a waitress – which would bruise my ego – but more, it wouldn't do me any good, given that, even if I worked all my life, on a waitress's salary I would never earn enough to pay off all the debts I have contracted since becoming better off.

One year, in Bordeaux, when I was living alone with my two children, I was so poor I had to give up the telephone, and I never bought anything but two thin slices of ham, one for Noé and one for Piero. I did without, I didn't mind. Occasionally, I did a bit of shoplifting, it didn't bother me, it was even fun. I had 'pleasure-shoplifting' trips, for underwear or presents, and 'practical-shoplifting' trips, for packets of nappies, for example. Either way, I simply wasn't able either to pay for the stuff, or do without it. Today, I wouldn't dare do it.

So that's how I lost a bit of my freedom. Because of myself: because I don't have the courage to not give a damn about what others think.

At that time of great material deprivation there were, all the same, other aspects of my life which were pure luxury: I went to the theatre and I had lovers.

Once, I found work as a census official. I was allocated a very poor neighbourhood, on the other side of town. I went there by bus when the kids were at school, or, on Saturdays, when Piero was having his afternoon nap – he was two years old and slept like an angel – and I took Noé with me.

There were lots of high-rise blocks, but also some very wretched houses, some without water or electricity. I had to brave Alsatians to get into people's homes, where I was sometimes received with extreme hospitality, sometimes with animosity, since they took me for someone from the government, or at least the council. I filled in my census forms (for each of which I was paid about one franc) on wax tablecloths still stained with red wine or coffee, and the list of a single mother's children would end up reduced to a list of prisoners.

After an hour and a half, Noé and I, hand in hand, would dash back to the bus stop, in order to get home to our little flat under the eaves in time for Piero waking up. From time to time, after telling Noé, I would go back in the evening, alone, while they both slept.

The train rolls on, through the window electricity cables cross and uncross to infinity. At Éralitz the cold is descending again on the little house in the snow, the cold is descending again on the black cardboard boxes containing my old journal, those notebooks in which the years unfold, where so many loves, thousands of emotions from everyday life struggle naïvely, on the cardboard boxes containing a jumble of old poems, one or two drawings, children's words and love letters, but I have lost so many . . .

The cold is descending on the hundreds of old books, on the two or three old objects, on the photo albums, on the memories which will now return to sleep, deep in my breast. Tomorrow perhaps I will remember nothing more than the lights of Marrakech, Iráklion or Stockholm, tomorrow perhaps I will be in Ouagadougou, Sydney or Saint Petersburg. Tomorrow, on my own, standing vibrant with joy in the middle of the room, I want to listen again to the *Magnificat* of Bach, which I sang as a child in a large choir, a pleasure without equal.

During our trip to the United States, we passed through a village called Truth or Consequences. When I saw the name on the map, I felt that our voyage had no other goal than to end up at this village. At once, this dot on the map became a sort of Eldorado, a fascinating, disquieting destination. Truth or consequences, was that what we were looking for?

So we decided that our route would go through Truth or Consequences. Of course it was a village like any other, except that it was deserted. It was a Sunday, and everything was closed. There was no one in the streets. We parked in the empty square. Since there was absolutely nothing doing, we got back in the car and continued our journey.

Leaving the village, however, we came upon a sign which gave a brief account of this strange

WHEN YOU LOVE YOU MUST DEPART

name. Truth or Consequences was the name of a radio programme back in the forties.

For weeks afterwards, I thought about this name. I couldn't work it out. What was the meaning of this *or*? Did it mean *or else*, as in *your money or your life: truth, or else the consequences*? Or did it mean *in other words*, as in *Justine, or the Misfortunes of Virtue*: *truth, in other words consequences*?

In the first case you could read it as saying, if you don't tell the truth, you must expect and suffer the consequences. You could just as well have said: *lie or (in other words) consequences*.

In the second case it is the exact opposite: if you tell the truth, you have to suffer the consequences.

I was intent on exploring the meaning of this sequence of three words, I tracked down the lie, I was sure that these three words spoke of the lie, but I couldn't locate the chink in their armour, it was a hermetically sealed sequence of words, maddening as a Chinese puzzle.

I was sure of only one thing, and that was, whichever way you read it, Truth or Consequences was a threat. Truth, whether expressed or concealed, was associated with a threat, a cunning, mysterious threat, since you did not

know either the nature of these proposed consequences, or what it was that would unleash
them. Contrary to the saying 'forewarned is
forearmed', these three words hung a sword of
Damocles over you, leaving you totally dis-
armed and powerless.

What was I afraid of? Perhaps the message of
this dot on the map was different for each individual. Perhaps, by obsessing me for all those
weeks, it was only trying to ask me, myself, to
face my own living truth in writing. Without
worrying too much about the consequences,
since, either way, truth or lie, the consequences threaten.

I must ask Oscar what that music is that he
put on his answerphone.
    The train is pulling into the station, I will
write the last word of this novel before I get
off.
    On the platform there will be women waiting
for men, men there to collect women, and fam-
ilies, business travellers, a whole crowd in a
hurry to find someone, something, get to the
underground, jump into a taxi, put down their
bags . . . And perhaps an adolescent girl, setting

off for the first time to discover the world . . .
She will not run, she doesn't know what is
awaiting her, she tells herself everything is
possible . . . My heart is beating like hers, like
her I think life is great and beautiful, and I
love it.